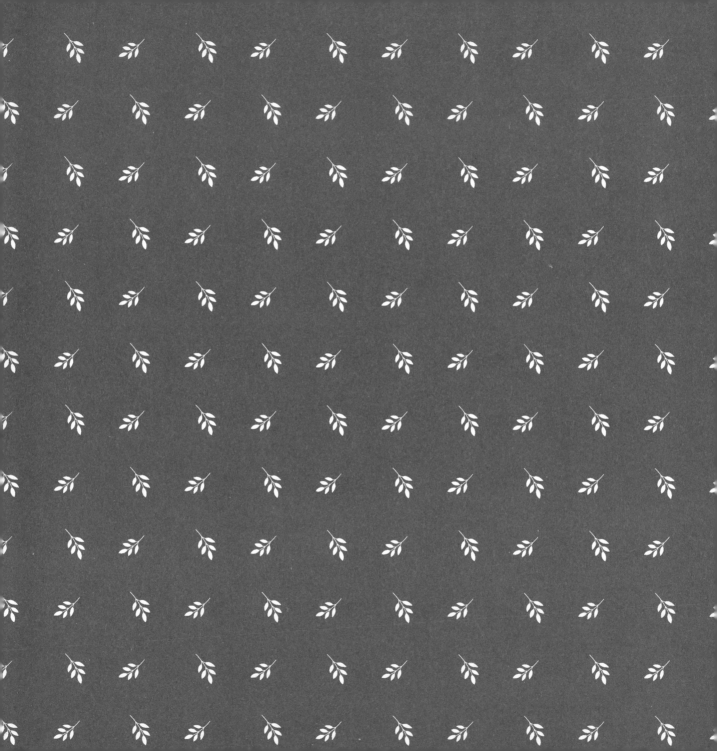

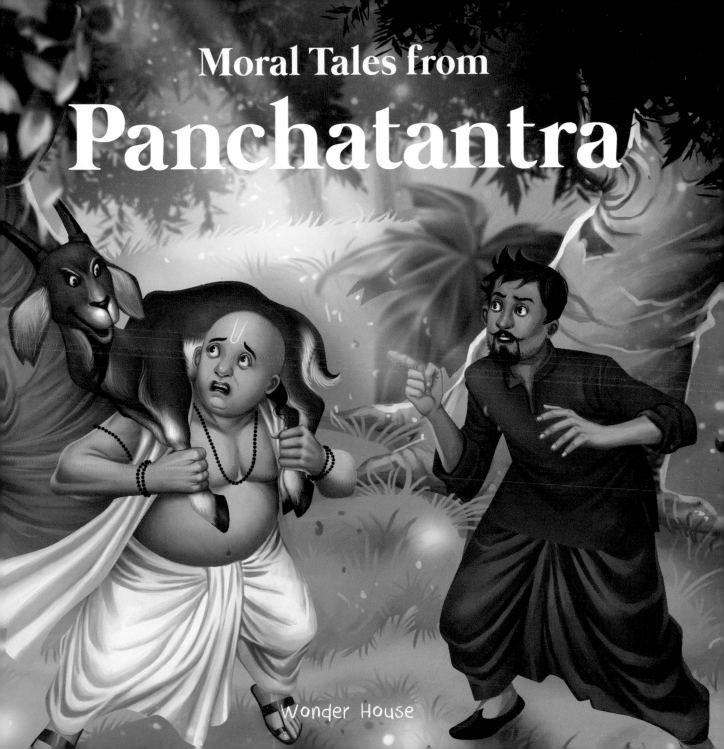

Moral Tales from
Panchatantra

Wonder House

Wonder House

(An imprint of Prakash Books)

contact@wonderhousebooks.com

ISBN : 978-93-89178-12-8

Contents

About Panchatantra

The Panchatantra is a collection of five books comprising ancient Indian fables written by Pandit Vishnu Sharma. It is believed to be composed somewhere in the 3rd century BCE. Panchatantra is based on *nitishastra*. The word 'Panchatantra' is made of two Sanskrit words, *pancha* (five) and *tantra* (thing). It talks about *mitra bheda* (estrangement of friends), *mitra samprapti* (winning of friends), *kakalukiyam* (of crows and owls), *labdha pranasam* (loss of gains), and *aparikshita karakam* (rash deeds). The work is spread across the globe. It first reached Europe sometime in the 11th century. It existed in various languages like Old Slavonic, German, Spanish, Latin, Greek, French and Czech.

In Franklin Edgerton's words, the Panchatantra is "certainly the most frequently translated literary product of India." The stories are as relevant in modern times as they were in the ancient times.

A long time ago, in ancient India, there was a beautiful kingdom named Mahilaropya. The kingdom was ruled by a king named Amarshakti. He had three sons named Ugrashakti, Bahushakti and Anantashakti. Being a scholar himself, Amarshakti was disappointed with his sons' disinterest in learning. Their laziness and inability to gain knowledge made the king very angry.

One day, he called his ministers to discuss with them the future of his successors. The king said, "I have called upon you to seek advice on an important matter. The men of learning say that idle sons bring dishonour to their father. And I have three of the laziest sons to worry about. I turn to you for counsel on this." One of the ministers came forward and advised the king to consult a wise Brahmin, Pandit Vishnu Sharma.

Amarshakti accepted his minister's advice and asked him to summon Vishnu Sharma to the palace.

When the Pandit arrived, the king addressed him, saying, "O gentleman, you must undertake the responsibility of teaching my sons. In return, I will grant you several acres of land." Vishnu Sharma smiled, "Oh king, I do not need your lands. Knowledge can't be purchased with money. I will tutor your sons. Six months from now, your sons will be great scholars. And if they are not, you can order me to change my name!" From that day onwards, the sons lived with Vishnu Sharma and learned the five books, *The Loss of Friends, The Winning of Friends, Crows and Owls, Loss of Gains,* and *Ill-considered Actions,* by heart.

The combination of these five books is known as *Panchatantra*. It is a *nitishastra*, also known as a 'textbook of ethics', which teaches the wise conduct of life. Each wise and witty story in all the five books teaches the harmonious development of humans and the ability to achieve joy by combining friendship, prosperity, security, action and learning. Since ancient times, Panchatantra has been regarded as a popular children's guide for solving problems of life and continues to do so even today.

We have selected six famous animal stories from the Panchatantra for children. The stories are accompanied with bright and beautiful illustrations to make reading a fun-filled experience for the child.

The Deer's Rescue

Once upon a time, a beautiful deer lived in the forest. Every afternoon, he went to a lake to meet his best friends.

His friends—a turtle, a crow and a mouse—patiently waited for the deer, near the lake. The four friends spent the afternoons sharing witty stories.

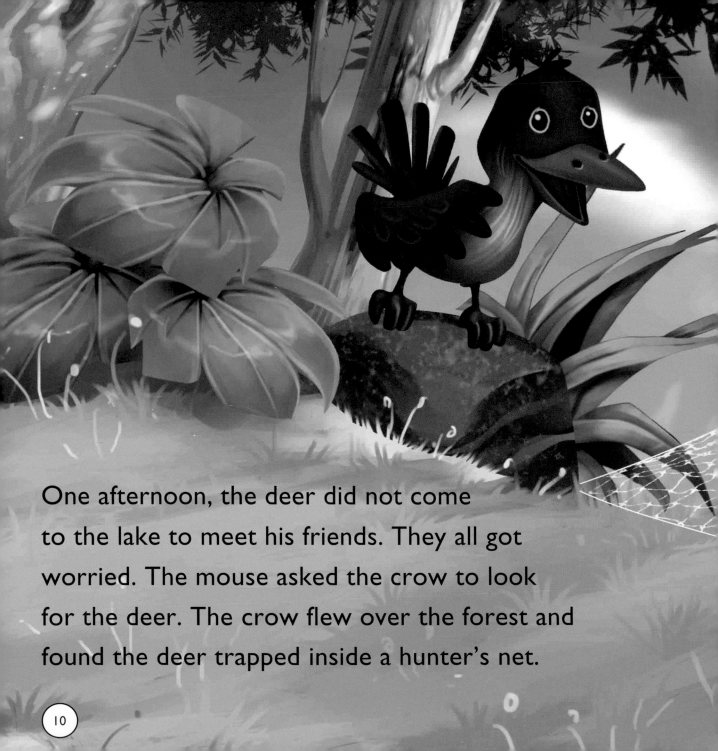

One afternoon, the deer did not come
to the lake to meet his friends. They all got
worried. The mouse asked the crow to look
for the deer. The crow flew over the forest and
found the deer trapped inside a hunter's net.

The crow approached the deer and said in a reassuring voice, "Do not worry, my dear friend! I'll come back with the mouse to cut this net and set you free."

The crow returned to the lake and narrated the troubling incident to the mouse and the turtle.

The mouse climbed on the crow's back and they flew back to rescue the deer. The mouse began to cut the deer's net swiftly.

The crow was shocked and worried when he saw the turtle walking slowly towards them.

He shouted at the turtle, "Go back! Your life is in danger! I can hear the hunter approaching."

The mouse chewed the wires of the net and set the deer free. When the hunter arrived, the deer ran swiftly into the forest, the mouse hid in a hole, and the crow flew high in the air.

However, the slow turtle couldn't escape. The hunter easily captured the turtle in a net. He slung it over his shoulder and started heading back home.

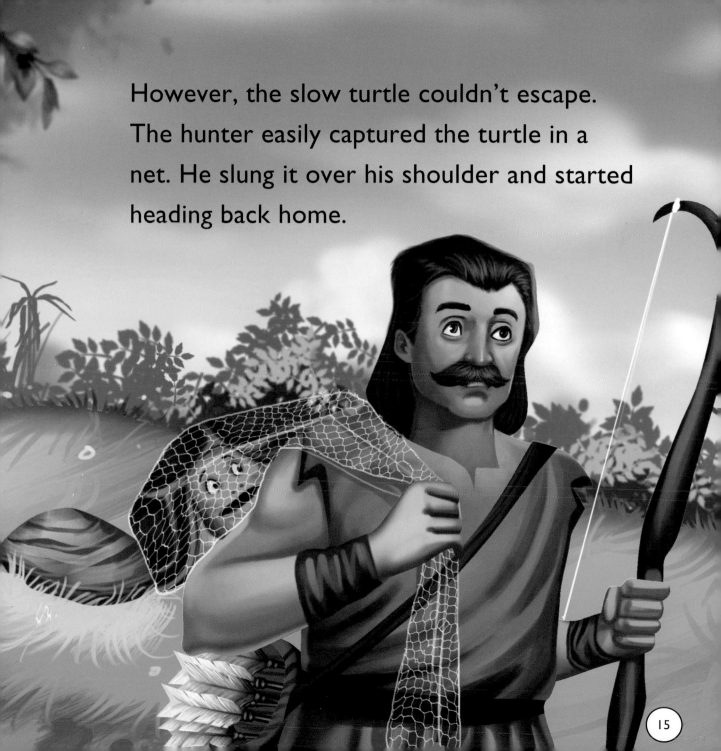

The deer, the mouse, and the crow came up with a plan to rescue their friend.

As the hunter approached the lake, the deer lay lifelessly on the ground, while the crow pretended to peck at its eye.

The hunter couldn't resist the opportunity to capture a dead deer. He put down the turtle, along with his belongings, and ran towards the deer.

The mouse quickly approached the turtle and chewed the net open with his sharp teeth. He urged the turtle, "Let's escape before the hunter returns. Go inside the lake and hide until it is safe to come out."

The turtle hid in the lake, while the mouse took shelter inside a hole in the ground. The crow was relieved to see that his friends were safe. He signalled to the deer.

The deer got up quickly and ran away, while the crow flew and sat on the highest branch of a tall tree. The disappointed hunter went back to fetch the turtle.

He was shocked to see the torn net. The four friends celebrated their escape as the hunter went back home empty-handed.

Moral
Teamwork can help overcome all obstacles.

The Dove and the Hunter

Once upon a time, there stood a large banyan tree in the forest. It was home to many species of birds and animals.

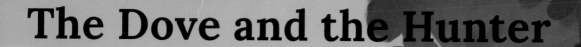

One day, a crafty hunter came to the forest to catch some birds. He laid a trap under the banyan tree and spread grains all over his net to lure the hungry birds.

A flock of doves spotted the delicious grains from the sky. But the king of doves was a wise bird. He suspected some foul play.

He sensed the danger and warned the doves, "Stop! It is a trap. How can so many grains appear at one place in the forest?" But the doves were extremely hungry and did not listen to their king. They landed on the ground to eat the grains.

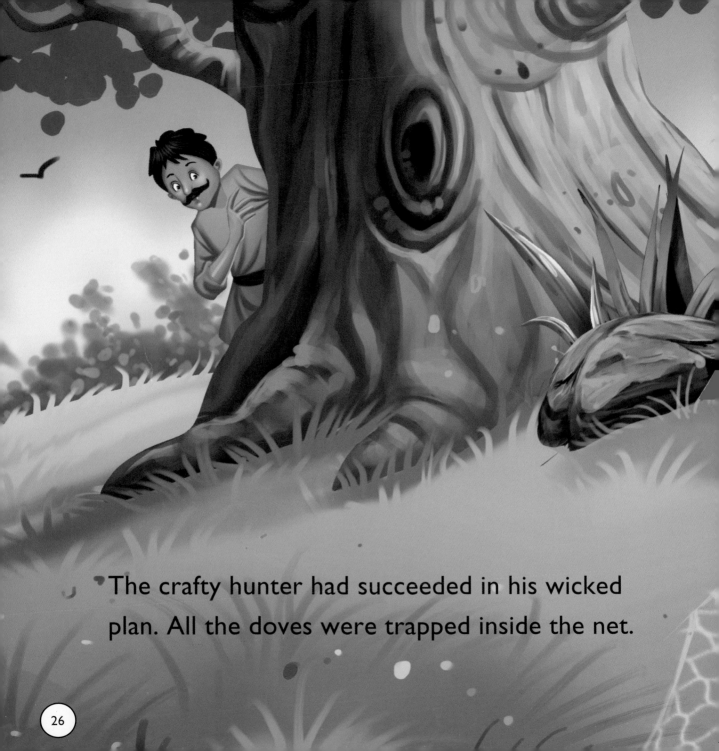

The crafty hunter had succeeded in his wicked plan. All the doves were trapped inside the net.

The doves got really scared and panicked. They started blaming each other for their misfortune. The hunter was pleased with the nice catch. He left to fetch a large cage for the birds.

The king of doves realised that they had only one opportunity to save their lives. He tried to calm everyone down and said, "Please listen to me, friends.

We can never free ourselves if we keep fighting with each other. We have to work together to escape from the hunter."

The doves agreed to listen to their king's plan.

The king instructed all the doves to fly together, towards the sky, while still inside the net.

All the doves followed their king's suggestion and flapped their wings together.

Soon, they were soaring high in the sky, taking the net along with them. The hunter could not believe his eyes and cursed his bad luck.

The king told his friends to fly in
the direction of the small hill at
the edge of the forest.

The birds landed near the house of a mouse.
The mouse came out of his hole when he heard
the king of doves call out his name.

The king requested the mouse, "Oh, dear friend!
We need your help in cutting down this net."

The mouse replied sadly, "I have grown old and my teeth are weak. I can free you, my friend, but I can't help the rest of the doves."

The king of doves said in a firm tone, "I can't abandon my subjects in distress. I prefer to stay trapped with them."

The mouse smiled and replied, "You have passed my test. You deserve to be a king."

The mouse cut down the net instantly and freed all the doves. The king of doves thanked the mouse.
The flock of doves flew back to their home.

Moral
Unity is strength.

The Brahmin and the Crooks

Many years ago, there lived a Brahmin who worshipped the God of Fire. One day, the Brahmin decided to perform a sacrificial ritual. He travelled to a nearby village to meet one of his devotees.

He asked the devotee to gift him a healthy goat for the holy sacrifice.

The devotee gladly fulfilled the Brahmin's wish by giving him his best goat.

The Brahmin carried the goat on his shoulders and started heading back home. On his journey through the forest, three crooks spotted him with the goat.

One of the crooks said to the others, "Can you imagine how delicious that goat must be?"

The second crook said wickedly, "I have a plan to steal that goat from the Brahmin. Listen carefully..."

The first crook took the shorter road and stood in the Brahmin's path. When the Brahmin approached him, the crook asked, pretending to be surprised, "What is wrong with you, Brahmin? Why are you carrying a dog on your shoulders?"

He scolded the crook for his bad eyesight and continued walking.

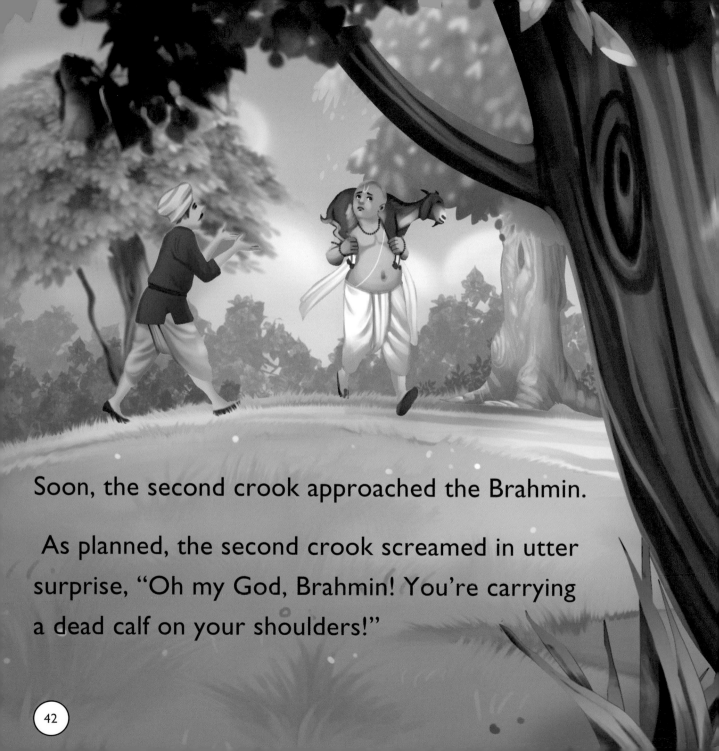

Soon, the second crook approached the Brahmin.

As planned, the second crook screamed in utter surprise, "Oh my God, Brahmin! You're carrying a dead calf on your shoulders!"

This time, the Brahmin was confused and looked at the animal on his shoulders.

Once he was convinced that it was the same goat he had been carrying all along, he scolded the second crook for his poor vision too.

The Brahmin had not walked much farther before the third crook crossed his path.

The third crook looked at the Brahmin with disbelief and said, "Why are you carrying a donkey on your shoulders?"

By now, the Brahmin was convinced that he was actually carrying a shape-changing demon on his shoulders.

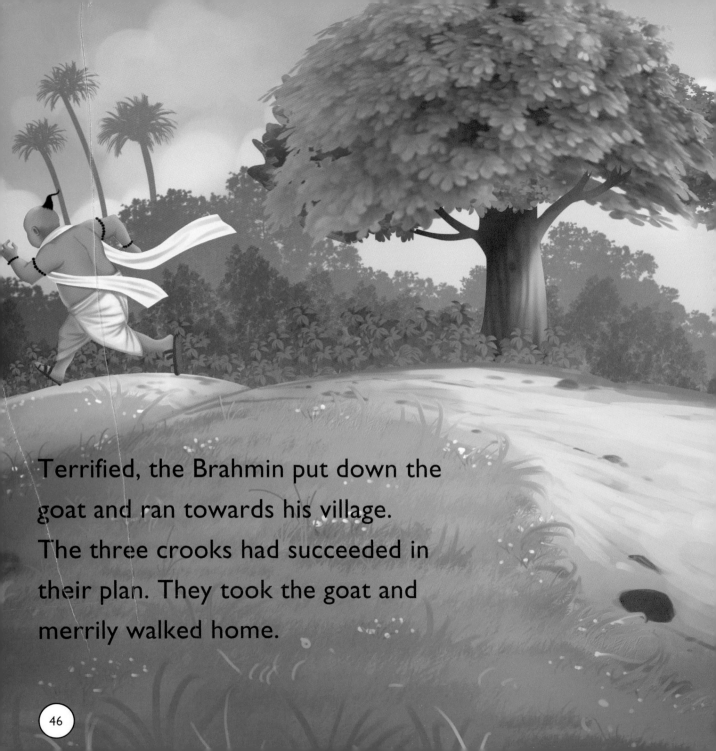

Terrified, the Brahmin put down the
goat and ran towards his village.
The three crooks had succeeded in
their plan. They took the goat and
merrily walked home.

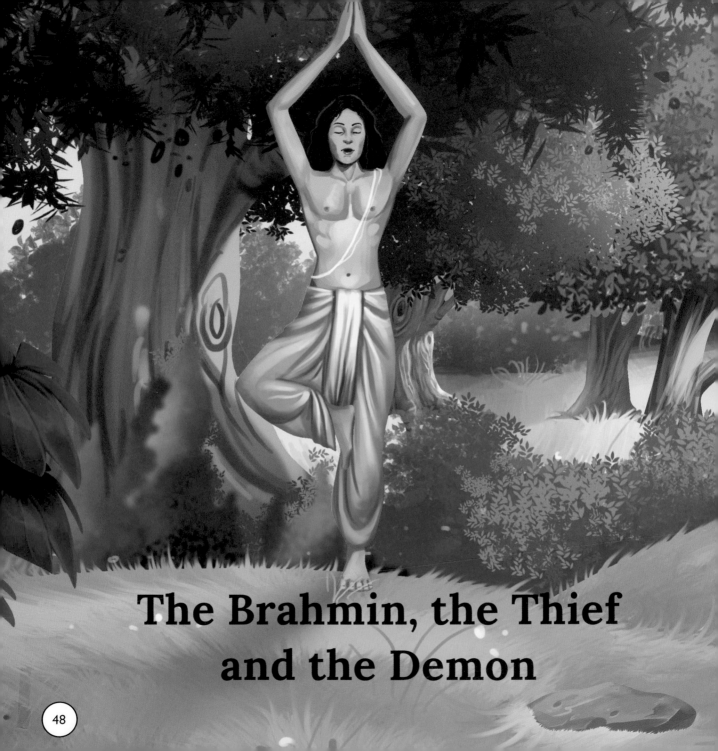

The Brahmin, the Thief
and the Demon

In ancient India, there lived a Brahmin named Drona, who had renounced all the luxuries of life. He followed rigorous practices of worship, which left him lean and weak.

A rich devotee gifted Drona two young calves
to show his respect and gratitude.

The Brahmin became fond of these calves and took great care of them as if they were his own children. Within no time, the calves grew fat and healthy.

One day, while on his way to the forest, a thief noticed the Brahmin's healthy calves and planned to steal them during the night.

At dusk, the thief was on his way to the Brahmin's cottage, when a giant demon stopped him. The demon asked in an authoritative voice, "Where are you going? Tell me the truth or I'll eat you right now!"

The thief was terrified. He told the demon about his plan.

After thinking a lot, the demon said, "Take me with you! You can steal those calves while I eat that Brahmin in his sleep."

The thief and the demon reached the Brahmin's hut and waited for him to fall asleep.

Once the Brahmin fell asleep, the demon rushed to kill him. Fearing that the demon might wake up the Brahmin, the thief suggested that the demon should wait until he had stolen the calves.

But the demon was adamant. He said, "I will eat the Brahmin first, as the noise made by the calves might wake him up."

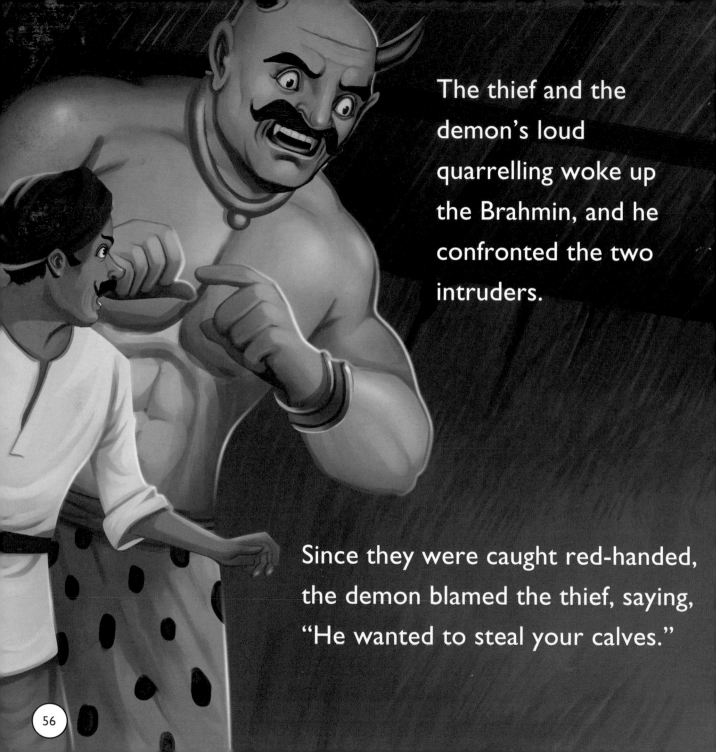

The thief and the demon's loud quarrelling woke up the Brahmin, and he confronted the two intruders.

Since they were caught red-handed, the demon blamed the thief, saying, "He wanted to steal your calves."

The thief retorted angrily, "The demon wanted to eat you alive!"

The Brahmin said, "How dare you? I will curse you! Om…"

The demon was scared of curses and ran away quickly. Once the Brahmin got rid of the demon, he chased the thief away with a large stick. The Brahmin and his calves never saw the thief or the demon again.

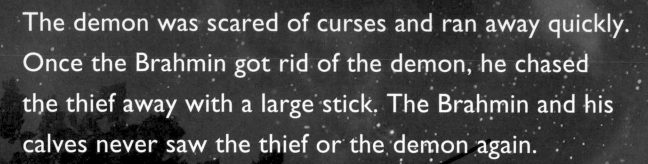

The Cave that Talked

Once, a lion spent the entire day hunting in the forest but could not find any prey. He was tired and grumpy, when he spotted a cave.

The lion thought to himself, "I should wait inside the cave. Whenever an animal comes in, I can eat it."

Soon, a jackal approached the cave. He spotted the footprints of a lion going inside the cave; but none of him coming out.

To be safe, the smart jackal said, "Oh mighty cave! Is it safe to come inside?" There was silence. He spoke again, "Don't forget, I can't enter unless you tell me to!"

The jackal's odd behaviour confused the lion. He thought to himself, "Maybe this is a magical cave that talks to its master. It is possible that it's not replying to the jackal because I'm already inside the cave.

The jackal will not enter
the cave until the cave
replies to him."

65

The lion wanted the jackal to come
inside the cave as soon as possible,
so he could satisfy his hunger.

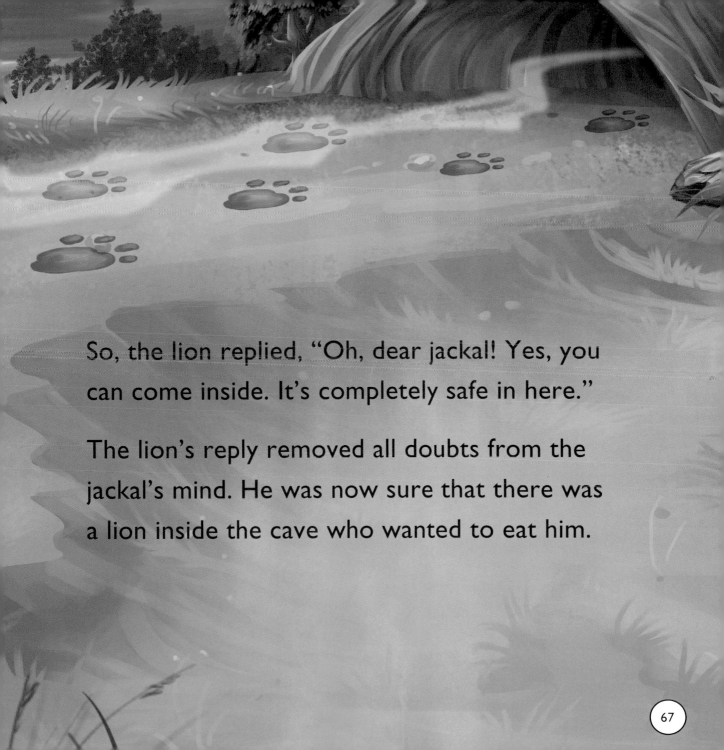

So, the lion replied, "Oh, dear jackal! Yes, you can come inside. It's completely safe in here."

The lion's reply removed all doubts from the jackal's mind. He was now sure that there was a lion inside the cave who wanted to eat him.

The smart jackal ran away from the cave to save his life.

The dejected lion finally left the cave when he realised that he had been fooled by the jackal.

The foolish lion remained hungry for a long time.

Moral
Think before you speak.

The Wedding of the Mouse

One fine morning, a learned sage was bathing in the holy water of River Ganges.

He was absorbed in his morning prayers,
when a little mouse landed in his hands.
The sage looked up and realised that
the wounded mouse had fallen out of an
eagle's grasp. He healed the mouse with
his powers.

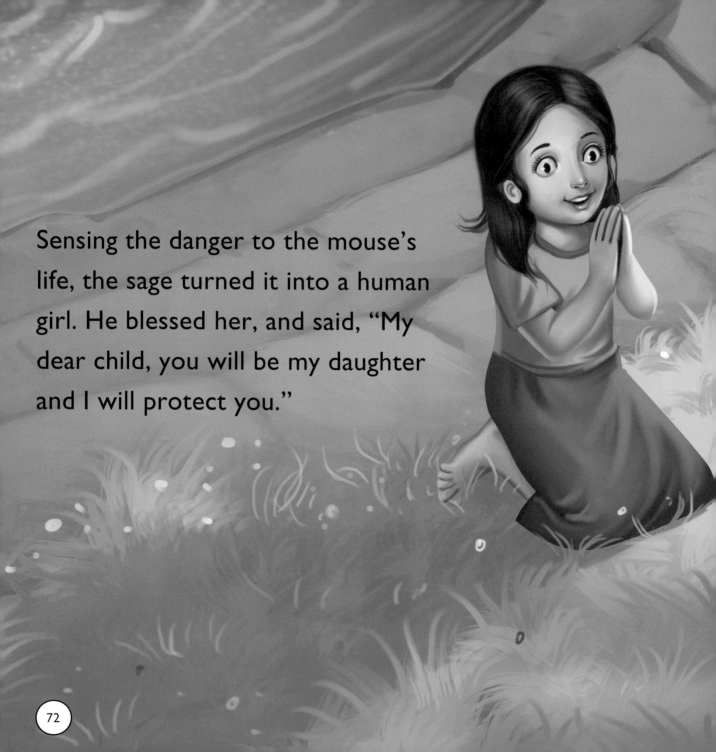

Sensing the danger to the mouse's life, the sage turned it into a human girl. He blessed her, and said, "My dear child, you will be my daughter and I will protect you."

The sage took the girl to his ashram and narrated the incident to his wife. The sage and his wife raised the girl as their daughter and showered her with love and affection.

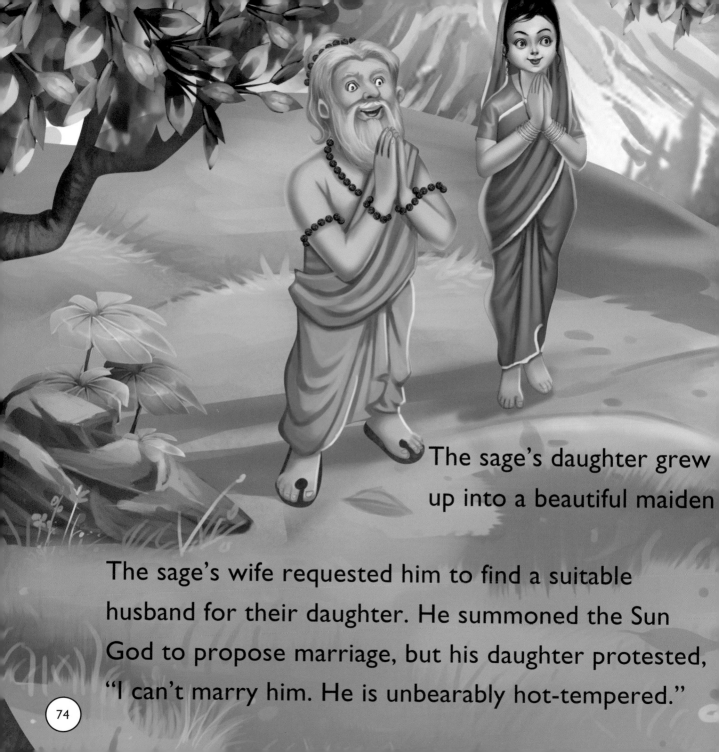

The sage's daughter grew up into a beautiful maiden

The sage's wife requested him to find a suitable husband for their daughter. He summoned the Sun God to propose marriage, but his daughter protested, "I can't marry him. He is unbearably hot-tempered."

The Sun God suggested, "Speak to the King of Clouds. He is the only one who can dim my light."

The sage summoned the King of Clouds. However, the daughter rejected him too, saying, "He is too dark, wet and cold. I do not wish to marry him."

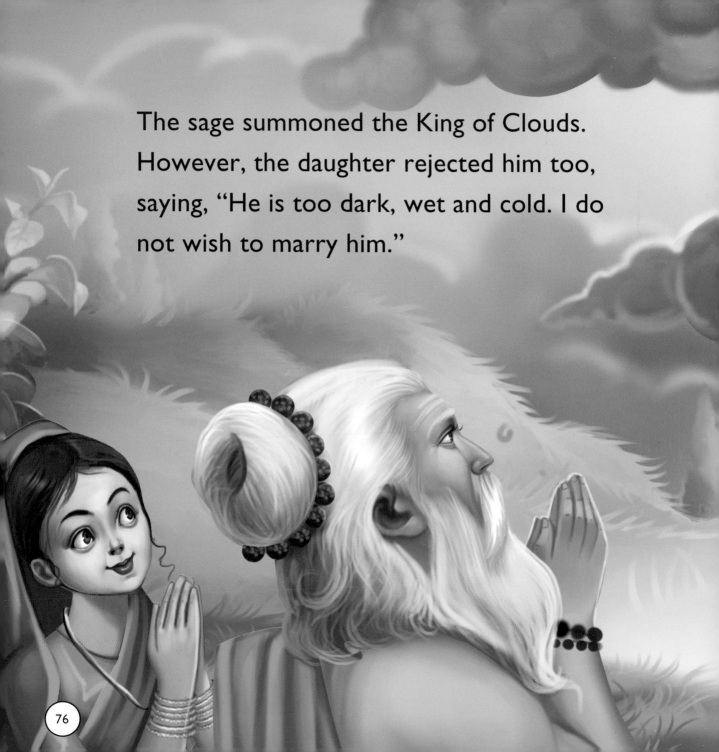

The King of Clouds said,
"The Lord of Mountains is superior to
me. He can stop me from blowing.

You should consider him for
your daughter."

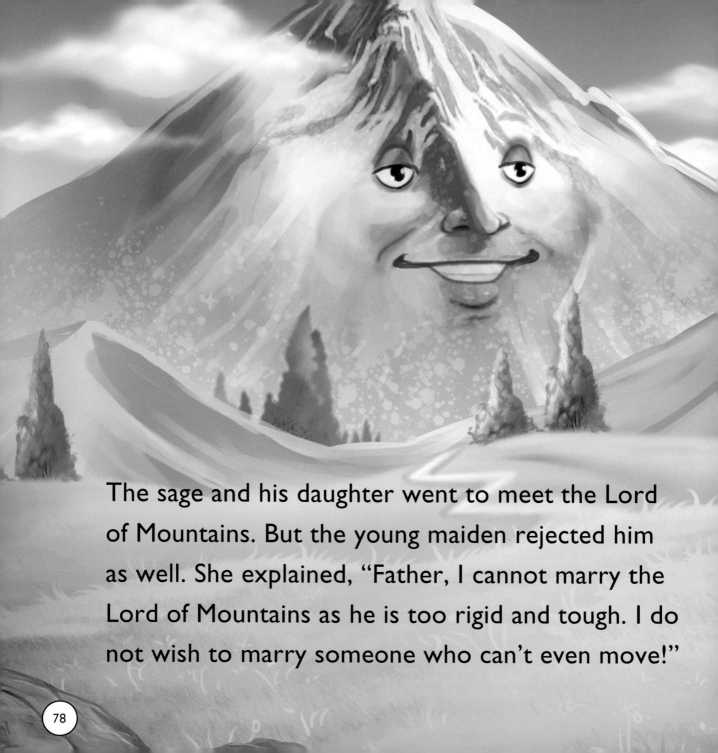

The sage and his daughter went to meet the Lord of Mountains. But the young maiden rejected him as well. She explained, "Father, I cannot marry the Lord of Mountains as he is too rigid and tough. I do not wish to marry someone who can't even move!"

The Lord of Mountains humbly said, "The King of Mice is even superior to me as he can dig holes inside mountains. You should go to him with your proposal."

Finally, the sage and his daughter arrived at a hillside and summoned the King of Mice.

The sage introduced his daughter to the King of Mice and said, "I am looking for a suitable husband for my daughter. Will you marry her?"

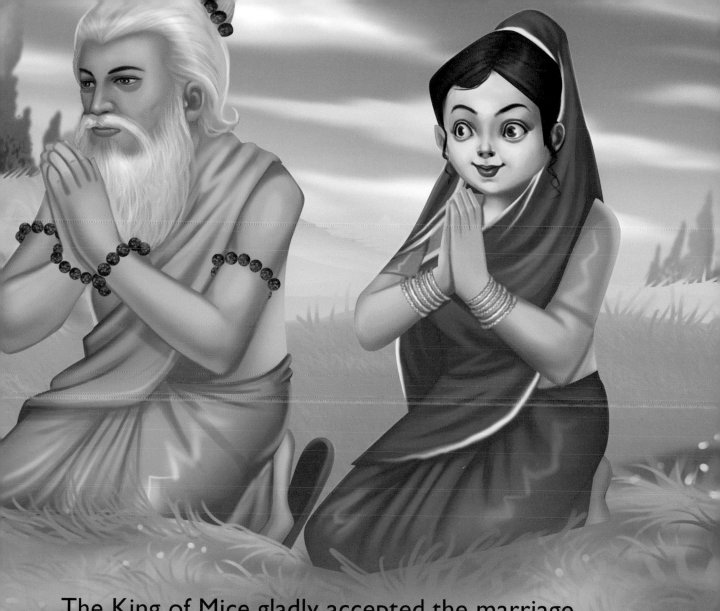

The King of Mice gladly accepted the marriage proposal. The sage's daughter was also delighted to see the King of Mice and agreed to marry him.

The sage transformed his daughter back into
a beautiful mouse and made preparations for
their wedding. The sage's daughter and the
King of Mice were married in a royal ceremony.
The sage blessed the couple and left.

The End

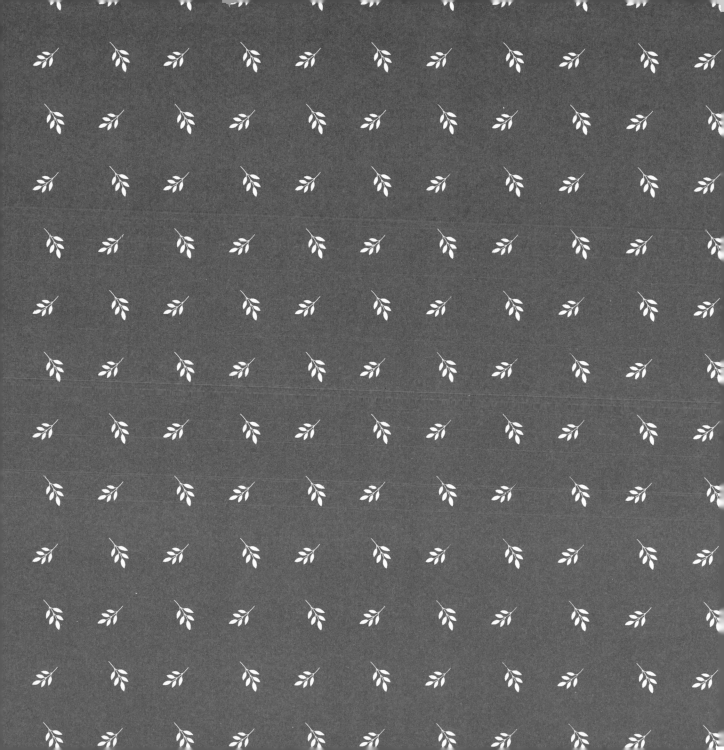

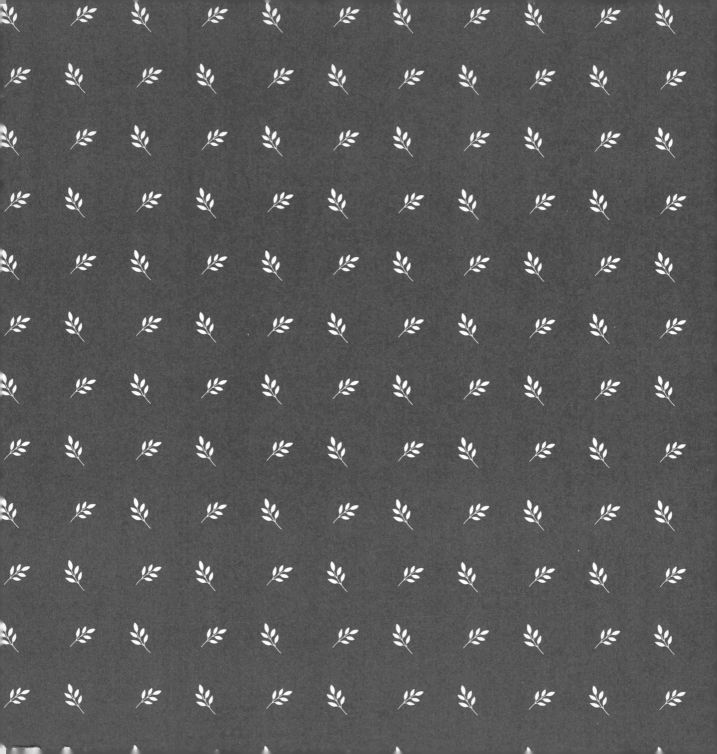